SONIC X™

W9-ATK-157

by P.J. Rudi

Meteor Shower Messenger

Grosset & Dunlap

GROSSET & DUNLAP
Published by the Penguin Group
Penguin Group (USA) Inc., 375 Hudson Street, New York, New York 10014, U.S.A.
Penguin Group (Canada), 10 Alcorn Avenue, Toronto, Ontario, Canada M4V 3B2
(a division of Pearson Penguin Canada Inc.)
Penguin Books Ltd, 80 Strand, London WC2R 0RL, England
Penguin Ireland, 25 St Stephen's Green, Dublin 2, Ireland
(a division of Penguin Books Ltd)
Penguin Group (Australia), 250 Camberwell Road, Camberwell, Victoria 3124, Australia
(a division of Pearson Australia Group Pty Ltd)
Penguin Books India Pvt Ltd, 11 Community Centre, Panchsheel Park, New Delhi – 110 017, India
Penguin Group (NZ), Cnr Airborne and Rosedale Roads, Albany, Auckland 1310, New Zealand
(a division of Pearson New Zealand Ltd)
Penguin Books (South Africa) (Pty) Ltd, 24 Sturdee Avenue, Rosebank,
Johannesburg 2196, South Africa

Penguin Books Ltd, Registered Offices:
80 Strand, London WC2R 0RL, England

If you purchased this book without a cover, you should be aware that this book is stolen property. It was reported as "unsold and destroyed" to the publisher, and neither the author nor the publisher has received any payment for this "stripped book."

The scanning, uploading, and distribution of this book via the Internet or via any other means without the permission of the publisher is illegal and punishable by law. Please purchase only authorized electronic editions, and do not participate in or encourage electronic piracy of copyrighted materials. Your support of the author's rights is appreciated.

© SONIC Project

Used under license by Penguin Young Readers Group. Published in 2005 by Grosset & Dunlap, a division of Penguin Young Readers Group, 345 Hudson Street, New York, New York 10014. GROSSET & DUNLAP is a trademark of Penguin Group (USA) Inc. Printed in the U.S.A.

Library of Congress Cataloging-in-Publication Data

Rudi, P. J.
  Meteor shower messenger / by P.J. Rudi.
      p. cm.
  Summary: Sonic scatters the Chaos Emeralds to the far reaches of space to protect them from Dark Oak, then must battle the Metarex, a robot monster that wants to destroy the Earth.
  ISBN 0-448-43996-4
  [1. Heroes—Fiction. 2. Robots—Fiction. 3. Science fiction.] I. Title.
  PZ7.R873Met 2005
  [Fic]—dc22
                          2005010362

10 9 8 7 6 5 4 3 2

The Battle
for the
Chaos
Emeralds

A bright blue light streaked through space.

It wasn't a shooting star. It wasn't a comet. In fact, it wasn't anything that was normally found in space at all.

It was Super Sonic. He was in the middle of a fierce battle.

Super Sonic had already fought an army of Metarex robot monsters. Now it was time for him to take on his enemy, Dark Oak.

Dark Oak was after the Chaos Emeralds. This was nothing new. Super Sonic was ready to protect them, no matter what it took.

Super Sonic fought well, but he was getting

Super Sonic plunges through space!

tired. His glow began to dim. His super strength was weakening.

In the end, Super Sonic couldn't hold off his enemy any longer.

"It's no use," said Dark Oak. "Just hand the Chaos Emeralds over."

Super Sonic knew he could not win the battle. He also knew that he could not hand the Chaos Emeralds over to his enemy. So Super Sonic did the only thing that he could do.

"Chaos Control!" Super Sonic yelled.

The Chaos Emeralds surrounded Super Sonic. They shined brightly in the darkness of space. It was now or never.

With the last of his super strength, Super Sonic flung the Chaos Emeralds out in seven different directions.

Even though the Chaos Emeralds were no longer in his control, Super Sonic knew that they were safe from his enemy.

Dark Oak could only watch as the Chaos Emeralds disappeared. He could not believe what Super Sonic had done. The Chaos Emeralds had almost been within his grasp.

Super Sonic was glad to know that he had ruined Dark Oak's plans. With the Chaos Emeralds safe, he could finally rest.

He was exhausted.

Super Sonic let the last of his energy drain as he fell through space. The fight may have ended, but the battle was not over.

Dark Oak had many other allies throughout space. They could help him find the Chaos Emeralds.

He sent a message to his friends telling them to search for the Chaos Emeralds. It was top priority.

Then he switched to Phase Two of his battle plan.

"Dispatch the raid battalion," he ordered the Metarex. "Seize the Planet Egg of the planet in question!"

The Metarex went down to Sonic's home world in search of something called the Planet

Dark Oak and the Metarex eyes watching on!

Egg. Super Sonic continued to fall to his home planet. He had finally run out of energy. He was too tired to stop himself.

Super Sonic's powers drained from his body as he returned to normal.

He was just regular Sonic again by the time he crashed into the sea.

The Starry Sky

Meanwhile, on another part of Sonic's home planet, his friends were looking forward to an **exciting night.** But they didn't know how exciting it was going to be.

"Tails, can't you see anything yet?" Cream asked.

"Nope, but wait a little longer," Tails said. He looked through the lens of his video camera. "Maybe when it gets a bit darker we'll be able to see more."

According to the records from days of old, tonight was the night they would be able to see a **meteor shower.** Hundreds of shooting stars were going to fill the sky.

Tails had gathered with Amy, Cream, and Cheese to enjoy the view. Amy wished Sonic were there to share it with her.

"**Here it comes!**" Amy cheered as she saw the first shooting star.

"I'm going to start taping it," Tails said. He pressed the Record button.

Shooting stars filled the sky. But something didn't look quite right.

"Does that star look strange to you ?" Amy asked. She was pointing at a meteor. It wasn't flying with the others.

"It seems to be falling toward us!" Cream said.

Cream was right. The meteor was headed right for them.

It passed above their heads and crashed into the forest. Tails, Amy, Cheese, and Cream hurried through the forest to the spot where the meteor crashed. It wasn't hard to find. The meteor had crashed through the trees. It left a path that was easy to follow.

Sonic's friends approached the crater carefully. Smoke was rising out of the hole. They didn't know what they might find inside.

It turned out to be the last thing any of them expected.

"There's someone lying in the hole," Amy said.

The girl at the bottom of the crater let out a moan. She was alive, but she had been through a rough landing.

Amy sprang into action. "Your house is closest, Cream. We've got to get her help right away."

"I'll go tell Mother about this," Cream said, hurrying home.

Tails looked back up at the sky, amazed. "This girl probably came from outer space."

Tails helps the
mystery girl

Rescued

But the girl wasn't the only one to come crashing down from outer space that day.

Sonic was waking up on another part of the planet.

He was no longer in the sea. He was in somebody's bed.

"So, you've finally come to," a familiar voice said.

"Eggman?" Sonic said.

Sonic sprang out of bed when he realized he was in the home of another one of his enemies. The day had gone from bad to worse.

"How did I get here?" Sonic asked. The last thing he remembered was falling

"How did I get here?"

"You were pretty badly hurt."

from space. Everything after that was a total blank.

Sonic listened while Eggman told his story.

The story began when Eggman was out for his daily run.

"You were pretty badly hurt," Eggman said, "and lying on the beach."

Sonic tried to remember washing up on the beach, but he couldn't.

"I don't know what happened," Eggman said. "But I sure don't want to get up one morning and find you dead in the vicinity of my home."

Sonic didn't think Eggman was very funny.

"Be grateful I'm merciful enough to save my enemy's life," Eggman said.

"It is indeed noble to show such humanity to an enemy," Becoe said. He was one of Eggman's henchmen.

"I don't really understand why, though," Decoe said. Eggman's other henchman was easily confused.

"How come you were beat up like that?"

Bokkun asked. He was carrying a mug of cocoa for Sonic.

"I've gotta go!" Sonic said.

As Sonic hurried off, he ran into Bokkun and spilled some of the cocoa.

"Oh, sorry," Sonic said. "But I really gotta go!"

Sonic was always hurrying off to places.

"Thanks, Eggman!" Sonic said as he disappeared.

"He's just as rude as ever!" Decoe said when Sonic was gone.

"Can't he show more appreciation by treating us to a meal or something?" Becoe asked.

"Right," Decoe agreed.

"He's right, right!" Bokkun added. "Treat us to cake, Sonic!"

But Sonic was too far away to hear.

Eggman wasn't thinking about cake, though. He was wondering what Sonic was up to.

Strange Visitors

The mysterious stranger from space was safely tucked into bed at Cream's house. Unlike Sonic, she was still asleep.

As she slept, she had horrible dreams.

She was on her home planet. It was about to be destroyed.

She was running for her life.

A huge robot monster was after her. It was destroying everything in its path.

When she turned, she saw the monster's eyes glowing in the smoke. It was a truly scary sight.

"Cosmo! Run!" a woman was yelling to her.

But Cosmo couldn't move. She was frozen

Cosmo has a horrible dream

in fear.

The nightmare ended before the monster got her.

Cosmo woke from the nightmare to find herself in a room full of strangers.

"Ow," she said as she tried to get up. She was still hurting from the crash.

"Don't push yourself," Amy said. "You fell out of the sky."

"Did you come from another planet?" Cream asked.

Cosmo slowly nodded her head.

"There's somebody called Sonic on this planet, isn't there?" Cosmo asked. "I've come because I have something to tell him."

Sonic's friends introduced themselves to Cosmo. Then they heard a horrible noise.

They rushed to the window. The noise was coming from outside. It was above them, up in the sky.

Even though she was hurt, Cosmo got out of bed. She thought the noise sounded familiar.

She hoped that she was wrong.

But when she got to the window, she knew she wasn't wrong.

It was something that she had seen before...

Cosmo meets Sonic's friends

Path of Destruction

The Metarex passed Angel Island, floating in the sky.

Knuckles was resting in front of the Master Emerald, keeping it safe.

The noise from the Metarex woke him. He was used to seeing strange things, but this was different.

"An iron monster?" Knuckles asked. It was a very strange thing indeed.

From where he was standing, Knuckles could hear the Metarex speaking.

It said, "In search of Planet Egg. Will launch salvaging activity."

Knuckles was even more shocked by what it

The Metarex
destroys the trees

did next.

"It's trying to destroy the forest!" he yelled.

The Metarex shattered the trees as it landed. Its eyes began to glow. It was the same glow that Cosmo had seen in her nightmare.

Then the Metarex began its attack.

The beam dug up the ground and knocked over trees. Smoke filled the forest as the Metarex continued the destruction.

"Hey! Cut that out!" Knuckles yelled down to the iron monster.

But the monster didn't listen. It just continued its attack.

Knuckles had to act quickly. He didn't know what the iron monster was up to, but it was clear that it was up to no good.

If Knuckles didn't stop it, the entire forest would surely be destroyed.

The Attack

Knuckles left Angel Island and attacked the iron monster.

He moved quickly, throwing a punch at the Metarex in mid-air. But Knuckles was the one that was shocked by the punch. The Metarex hardly even noticed.

The Metarex waved its arm at Knuckles and flicked him aside.

"Whaaaaaaaa!!" Knuckles yelled as he flew through the air.

Knuckles landed on his feet in the forest. He knew he couldn't take on the robot monster alone.

Luckily, help came from above.

The missiles attack

A missile was flying toward the Metarex. Knuckles hoped that it would have better luck than he had.

More missiles flew toward the Metarex. They exploded, one after the other, hardly making a dent in the robot.

Knuckles looked up in the sky. The missiles were coming from the X-Tornade.

Tails was piloting the ship. He joined the attack.

"Tails, what is that thing?" Knuckles asked.

"I don't have the slightest idea," Tails replied.

"Back me up," Knuckles said. "I'm going to stop it."

Tails prepared the X-Tornade for the fight. He looked back to his passenger, Cosmo. She had insisted on coming along for the ride.

"We're going into battle mode," he said. "Are you going to be okay with that?"

"Yes," she said. She was even more prepared than he knew.

Tails swung the X-Tornade around to get a

better shot at the Metarex.

He fired the Vulcan at the huge target.

Amy, Cream, and Cheese ran to watch the battle. They could not believe what they were seeing. The forest was being destroyed. The Metarex was hardly scratched by the Vulcan.

"That girl seems to know about the robot," Amy said.

And she was right.

From inside the X-Tornade, the fight was not looking good.

"The attacks have no effect," Tails said. He watched as the machine swatted Knuckles away again.

"Normal attack methods won't work on a Metarex," Cosmo said.

"What is that thing?" Tails asked.

Cosmo had trouble getting the words out. "It is . . . something that takes the life of planets . . . a machine version of Death."

The Metarex can't
be destroyed

The Battle Rages On

Just when it appeared that nothing could hurt the Metarex, a familiar blue streak of light flew past the X-Tornade. It crashed into the Metarex, sending the iron monster to the ground.

"Sonic!" his friends cheered as they watched from the ground. They knew that Sonic could take out this new enemy. Sonic had won many battles before.

Cosmo stood up in the X-Tornade to get a better look at Sonic. She was so excited that she even bumped her head.

"So, that's Sonic," she said. He was the reason she had come to the planet.

He was the only one that could stop the Metarex.

Sonic took a moment to look over the situation.

The Metarex may have fallen to the ground, but it was definitely not about to give up. The robot monster had managed to do a lot of damage. It looked like it had a lot more fight in it, too.

But Sonic wasn't really worried. He wasn't worried at all.

"You go all out, don't you?" he said to the machine. He flashed a cocky smile.

The Metarex was getting back up faster than Sonic had expected.

"Sonic!" Tails yelled as the X-Tornade emitted the ring.

"I got it!" Sonic yelled back as he grabbed the ring.

Sonic could feel his power grow as soon as he touched the ring. With new strength he started a spinning attack. He struck the Metarex in the chest and knocked the monster back.

Sonic grabs the ring

Sonic continued his spinning attack on the monster.

Suddenly, the Metarex swung its smaller arms at Sonic. Robot arms were everywhere, but Sonic managed to avoid being hit.

Knuckles joined in the attack, punching the Metarex while Sonic distracted it.

Neither Sonic nor Knuckles seemed to make a dent in the iron robot.

Eventually the Metarex was able to hit them back.

Sonic and Knuckles went crashing to the ground.

"My attacks aren't working," Knuckles said.

"He is unexpectedly tough," Sonic agreed.

Nothing that Sonic and Knuckles did could get through the machine's defenses. Its body armor was just too strong.

"Sonic, use the Chaos Emeralds," Knuckles said.

"Sorry!" Sonic replied. "The Chaos Emeralds are all the way beyond outer space."

Sonic explained that he had been forced to scatter the Emeralds to keep them safe.

Knuckles was not happy to hear that there were no Chaos Emeralds in the world just when he and Sonic really needed them.

Knuckles goes down

Planet Egg

The Metarex continued its attack. Sonic and Knuckles couldn't keep up with the robot's arms and laser beams. For a moment, they were lost in all the smoke.

The Metarex stretched out its arms. It was going straight for the planet's crust.

"Watch out!" Amy yelled as she pulled Cream out of the way.

Light shot out from the ground in front of the robot. The Metarex had found what it was looking for.

"For the tranquility and order of outer space!" the Metarex said.

The ground began to crack.

Pillars of light shoot out
from the ground

A huge chunk of the forest floor came up as the bright light grew.

"NOOOO!!" Cosmo yelled from inside the X-Tornade. She had seen this happen before. It was the cause of her nightmares.

Nothing could stop the Metarex. It was too strong.

Sonic and Knuckles could only watch helplessly as the bright light spread across the forest. Then they couldn't see anything except for that light.

The light finally dimmed. Sonic could see again. And he did not like what was before his eyes.

The Metarex had carved a deep chunk out of the ground. It found what it was looking for.

"What's that?" Tails asked.

"The Planet Egg," Cosmo replied. "The very life of planets. Planets that lose their Planet Egg lose their life energy and die."

A Shock and a Surprise

"Collection completed," the Metarex said. "Break away!"

The Metarex grabbed the Planet Egg and started to fly off with it.

"Hold it!" Sonic said as he started another spinning attack. He had to stop the Metarex.

Sonic went after the robot. Once again, the Metarex swatted Sonic away as if he were nothing.

"I'm not letting it get away!" Tails yelled as he aimed the X-Tornade toward the Metarex.

The Metarex easily brushed off the attack.

The Metarex captures
the Planet Egg

Tails chased the Metarex as far as he could, but the ship couldn't keep up.

"It's no good!" Tails yelled. He was forced to back off. "I can't chase it all the way into outer space in this craft."

Tails noticed that Cosmo looked dizzy. She asked him to open the door to the ship. He tried to explain that they were really far up in the sky, but she didn't care.

When Tails opened the door for her, Cosmo did something totally unexpected...

She jumped out of the ship.

Cosmo floated gently to the ground where she met up with Sonic. He wasn't looking too good from the battle, but Cosmo hardly noticed.

"How do you do?" she asked. "My name is Cosmo. You're Sonic, aren't you?"

"Yes," he replied.

Cosmo smiled. "You're the only hero capable of controlling the miracle gemstones," she said. "The Chaos Emeralds. Please! I beg you. The Universe is in crisis."

Before Sonic could respond, he heard Tails calling out for him.

"Sonic! Knuckles!" Tails said as he reached them. "The Master Emerald is glowing!"

This was great news. The glow of the Master Emerald was a signal that a Chaos Emerald was close by.

The Master Emerald
is glowing!

The Reunion

Meanwhile, on Earth, Sonic's friend Chris had grown up. He was now eighteen years old.

Time moved differently on Earth than it did on Sonic's home world. Six years had passed since Sonic left Earth. In those six years, Chris had missed his friend very much.

Chris had completed the transmission pod. He wrote a letter to his family and friends telling them what he was about to do. He knew if he had told them in person, they would try to stop him.

Once Chris had finished the letter, he stepped into the pod. If everything went the way he planned, it would take him to Sonic.

Chris steps out
of the light

On Angel Island, the Master Emerald was glowing brighter than anyone had ever seen it do before. Suddenly Sonic and his friends could see a shape in the light.

It looked like a person.

As the light began to dim, they could see the person better. They could not believe their eyes.

Chris Thorndyke stepped out of the light.

But he didn't look like he was eighteen anymore.

He looked more like he was twelve.